To Pamela

Jeannie Flauman

Tomasina
and the Little Hall of Mirrors

by Jean Hamilton Pearman

Photography by Dana Hyde

A PERCENTAGE OF THE PROFITS GOES TO THE FRIENDS OF VERSAILLES

Tomasina and the Little Hall of Mirrors:a dollhouse fantasy/by Jean
Pearman;photography by Dana Hyde.First edition.

p.cm.Illustrated with photographs of dollhouse version of Hall of
Mirrors,Versailles,France.

SUMMARY:
This children's book tells the story of a little girl who wants to be a
princess.Louis XIV,when he was a child,teaches her how to be one.
This fairytale-like story will delight any little girl.

Dana Hyde has photographed pictures inside the Hall with dolls as characters.

   Audience: Ages 4 to 10
   ISBN 0979630339

Registration with Bowker by ISBN No. 978-0-9796303-3-0

Printed by Phibbs Incorporated
110 Edward St., St. Thomas, Ontario Canada

Design - Phibbs Incorporated

To our Granddaughters

May they all visit the
original
Hall of Mirrors
at Versailles.

Tomasina

About the Author

Jean Pearman lives in Bermuda, New York, and Palm Beach with her husband, Richard.

When he retired, "Jeannie" who had been in the fashion business, enjoyed her grandchildren so much that she decided to write children's books about miniatures, her passion.

"Tomasina and the Little Hall of Mirrors' is her second book. Her first was "My Malmaison" about her dollhouse. All the photographs for both books were done by her friend, an accomplished photographer, Dana Hyde.

About the Photographer

Dana Hyde is a New York based fine arts photographer. Her editorial credits include "House and Garden", "Travel and Leisure", and the "New York Times".

Her book credits include "My Kind of Garden", by David Hicks and "My Malmaison", by Jean Hamilton Pearman.

Dana lives in New York and Southampton. She has two children and four grandchildren.

Introduction

Two years ago my husband and I, members of the Wallace Collection in London, spent a weekend at Versailles.

As a result we commissioned Robert Dawson to build our Hall of Mirrors.

I would visit his studio and see how the room was progressing, sometimes taking my little granddaughter, Tomasina, with me.

How fascinated we were at all the intricate detail and how it was made.

We include Robert's story at the end of this book.

Special thanks goes to Charles Moulton, Bob Whitney and Catharine Green.

The dolls were borrowed from the Tiny Doll House in New York, a charming little store selling miniatures, about the last one of its kind in the world.

Now our Hall of Mirrors lives at our house in Florida, admired by all. I wrote this story, "Tomasina and the Little Hall of Mirrors", about this Hall and all the magic surrounding it.

Tomasina
and the Little Hall of Mirrors

Chapter 1

Hello, my name is Tomasina. I am five years old and I have a big secret. I will tell you what it is if you promise not to tell anyone.

Here it is: everyone thinks my dolls are just dolls, of Louis XIV and his friends but that's not true. My dolls come to life at night and play with me in my little Hall of Mirrors, a famous room from Versailles. Grandie, my grandmother, who loves everything French had a dollhouse made for me. It's a replica of the Hall of Mirrors in Versailles.

Grandie told me that Versailles is the biggest chateau in the world. It is in France. Louis the XIV, who was the most famous king of France, built it almost four hundred years ago. He loved splendor and everything grand and wanted to build the most beautiful building in the whole world.

His father had built a hunting lodge at Versailles, but Louis brought in great architects and landscape designers to change it. He added many large rooms and built gardens all around them. He named this palace-like chateau "Versailles" because it was in the town of Versailles.

The Hall of Mirrors was Louis's favorite room in the chateau. It is very large with high ceilings and hundreds of mirrors and chandeliers.

I am afraid to tell Mommy my secret about my dolls coming to life at night. She will think I am crazy. You see, my dolls and I play together and have so much fun. My fairy doll is my favorite. She plays with me too and does special magic.

Last night something amazing happened and I want to tell you all about it.

Chapter 2

I had gone to bed in my blue bedroom, snuggled up under my feather quilt. Daddy had read me a story about the Hall of Mirrors called "Louis XIV and His Court". Then he turned out the light. He thought I had gone to sleep.

But I had not because after he closed my door, my fairy doll flew down from the bookshelf. She has magical powers.

"Tomasina, Tomasina,' whispered the fairy, "Would you like me to make you tiny so you can fit inside your Hall of Mirrors and play with Louis XIV?   He is in there right now and wants to meet you and teach you how to be a real princess."

"But Louis is a grown - up king," I said. "Why would he want to play with me when I am just a little girl?" "It's true. He lived to be an old king and died with many great grandchildren. But tonight, he has come in miniature at his favorite age. He became dauphin, which means 'prince', when he as only five years old and his father died. He became king at thirteen. Please come with me and meet him. You will really like him." said the fairy.

"Of course, I will come." I said. "It was my wish to learn to be a princess from a real prince." Whoosh! Off I flew with the fairy into my little Hall of Mirrors.

I looked down and saw my fingers. They were the same size as the fairy's fingers. Now I was almost as small as my fairy doll.

Chapter 3

"I could hardly believe my eyes. There, standing before me was the famous Prince Louis XIV. But he wasn't an old king at all. He was young and handsome. He was not much taller than I am and was dressed in a silver suit with a hat. It had a large white plume on it. He had long ringlets of brown curls and was smiling at me.

"Bonjour, Tomasina" he said, bowing deeply and kissing my hand.

'Bonjour' means 'Hello' in French. I knew that word from Grandie.

"I have come back to your little Hall of Mirrors," said Louis. "How lucky I was to find it. I built the real one so many years ago. Then it was the only one in the world. I am so happy that you have a copy of it so you can enjoy my beautiful room."

"So am I," I said, "or else I would not get to meet you. I feel very lucky to meet a real prince. None of my friends have ever met one. Can you teach me how to be a princess? Can we go to a ball?"

"But of course I will teach you what I know" said Louis, his eyes twinkling as though he were thinking of something special. "In a few years I will be crowned King, then I will wear a crown."

"How did you learn to be a king?" I asked.

"Maman gave me some lead soldiers to play with once when I was sick. I used to play with them on my bed covers. I did not mind being sick in bed because I would play for hours with my soldiers. I made mountains with pillows and learned how to surround the enemy from all sides to win a battle. Then the enemy could not win and had to retreat. I made my lead soldiers march in a row, holding the French flag. Its' colors are red, white and blue. I even marched them outside."

"Just the same as the colors in the American flag," I said.

"I do not know what the American flag looks like. It was not designed when I was king. But the English flag was and it is red, white and blue too." Louis said.

"What else did you do to learn to be a king?" I asked.

"Well, I liked chasing ducks with my brother, Monsieur. He later became the Duc de Orleans but as a little boy

we called him 'Monsieur'. We played in the gardens and in the L' Orangerie, which was a large group of orange trees. No other chateau in France had orange trees. They were a delicacy. Our other trees were often clipped to look like animals and called topiaries. Later, I bought a real elephant and a real camel to put in the garden too.

Then the government of Venice, a city in Italy where people travel by boats on canals instead of streets, gave me three gondolas and even gondoliers, the drivers, to drive them. You can imagine how surprised French people were to see gondolas in France. My gardens at Versailles were unlike any gardens anywhere else in the world.

Monsieur and I loved jumping into the fountains and splashing each other. So when I grew up, I put over fifteen hundred fountains all around my gardens. The fountains sprayed water high up into the air. I had waterfalls made too.

We were also taught to ride ponies so we would be good hunters. We would be able to lead all our soldiers in a battle. We would pretend our riding crops were swords. Our dogs would chase after us with their tongues hanging out. Their names were Bonne, Tonne, and Nonne. I loved my dogs.

Poor Monsieur was never allowed to win any games. I was meant to win everything because I would one day be the king. No one was ever allowed to beat the king at any game no matter what! Poor Monsieur was better at billiards and fencing, two different games, than I was. But he always had to let me win. Billiards was one game we played. Fencing was the other. It must have been hard for Monsieur to always lose but he was taught to be a good sport so he never complained.

Here is a coin of me as King

Maman also had me sit and listen at meetings to learn to govern France. I sat with all the Parliament members, lords, marquises and dukes. I learned how to raise money to govern France. Years later when I needed money for a war, I had to melt down all my silver furniture in this room. The throne and tall flower stands, called torcheres. It made me very sad, but we needed the money for making guns.

Most importantly, I learned from the leaders to always tell the truth. It is hard for me to admit I am wrong, but I do. You must too, Tomasina."

I will, I promised to myself.

"There will be a big parade for my Coronation. I will carry this red hat with white plumes and wear this silver suit. Look at the soles of my shoes. See how they are red on the bottom of my feet. The soles will show when I am marching. People will see them. Only nobility, people with titles like kings and queens, dukes and duchesses, lords and ladies, are allowed shoes with red soles. The proper name for this color is crimson.

Maman says in the parade I must turn my head slightly to the left and then to the right and to nod slowly as I walk in the parade so that all the people can see my face. I must express my gratitude and love for my countrymen. You must learn to do this same thing Tomasina, if you want to behave like a princess. You need to notice people on all sides of you at all times."

"Okay. I will try" I said, and moved my head back and forth.

"The townsfolk will bow down to me and remove their hats as a gesture honoring the king. Men should always remove their hats for a lady or an important gentleman. The marching band will be in front of me and play the "Marselleise", which is the name of the French National Anthem.

"Oh, I am learning 'God Save the Queen' at school and Daddy has taught me 'The Star Spangled' Banner."

"Good," said Louis. "I do not know of them but it is very important to know your countries' songs. I am very excited about the parade and becoming the king".

Chapter 4

"Here is a hat for you, Tomasina. I will show you
how to walk correctly with your head held high like
a princess. You must always have very good posture
with your back straight like a stick."

I took my hat and slowly turned my head from the
left to the right, nodding, with my head held high
and my back straight.

"But Louis, what about my dress?" I cannot wear
my nightgown. I need my princess costume but it is
in my bedroom closet. What if we should go to
a ball?"

"Do not worry, Tomasina. I have a surprise for you,"
said Louis. He smiled and raised his eyebrows high.

But I did worry. What would I do if I met Louis's friends, all these grand people, in my nightgown? I would be so embarrassed and Louis would not be proud of me. I could not stand tall and keep my head held high when I did not feel well dressed."

"Here is a hat for you, Tomasina. I will show you how to walk correctly with your head held high like a princess. You must always have very good posture with your back straight like a stick."

I took my hat and slowly turned my head from the left to the right, nodding, with my head held high and my back straight.

"But Louis, what about my dress?"   I cannot wear my nightgown. I need my princess costume but it is in my bedroom closet. What if we should go to a ball?"

"Do not worry, Tomasina. I have a surprise for you," said Louis with a grin.

Then the magic fairy touched my shoulder. She always took care of me. "Voila! Look at yourself now, Tomasina." I looked down at my waist. In place of my white nightgown was my pink ballerina dress, my tutu.

How had she taken it out of the closet? The magic fairy had miraculously put the pink tutu on me. I was so happy that I did a little pirouette, a spin, which I had learned in ballet class.

I looked down at my feet and saw my ballet shoes. I felt prettier than I had in my nightgown but I knew I was still not correctly dressed for the famous Hall of Mirrors or a ball. All the other ladies would have on ball dresses. Grandie had shown me her ball dresses. They were long to the floor and very fancy. What should I do now? I did not want to hurt the fairy's feelings but I felt I was not dressed correctly for a ball.

Louis looked at me with his lips squeezed together.

"Tomasina, I have an idea. I am going to introduce you as the guest ballerina when we go to the ball. Come with me. Do not worry about not having on a ball dress for a ball. You will be the guest of honor, which is even better than being just another lady at the ball." Louis beamed.

What if I did not dance well? I thought. I had not practiced recently. I bit my lip. I crossed my fingers for good luck.

Chapter 5

Violins began to play. My eyes widened. "This is heaven " I exclaimed, smiling as a princess would do. "No, Tomasina, this is The Hall of Mirrors". Ahead of us on a stage, was the grand throne made of silver.

On the ceiling was a colorful painting.

"What is the painting on the ceiling?'I asked. "That is called a mural. It shows Hercules in his chariot crossing a river. People think it looks like me. Some people call me the Sun King." Louis seemed very proud of what he was saying.

The whole room smelled like perfume."Is there perfume sprayed everywhere?" I asked.

"No, my little friend, the room smells from flowers called hyacinths, roses, and lilies. " Twinkling lights from the massive chandeliers reflected in the mirrors too. Outside the windows fireworks burst high into the sky. What an amazing sight.

I looked to the left and saw on a long wall a table with food of every kind. Gold and silver plates held meats, goat, capon, lamb, duck and tongue.

"Come see this buffet, Tomasina. You must be hungry. My favorite dish is called a frog's cherry. It is the leg and spine of the frog, dipped in batter and fried. It is delicious. Please try one." Said Louis.

I looked at the frog's cherry. I did not want to eat a piece of a frog.

"No, thank you, Louis, but I love the flowers in the salad. Do they taste good too?"

"Yes", said Louis, "the chef decorates the salad with spring violets. Here, put one in your hair."

I took the little flower and stuck the violet behind my ear. Now I smelled good too.

I looked at all the vegetables piled high in a cone

shape. There were cucumbers, asparagus tips, and artichoke bottoms on lovely china plates. If I ate anything, I would eat these vegetables because Mommy liked me to eat them before I had anything sweet. Then Louis showed me the peas.

"See the peas, Tomasina, are from England and called petit pois. That means, 'little peas'in English. They are so popular now in France that I have my servants put a little bowl by my bed every night. My mother says petit pois will give me pleasant dreams." I hope you dream of me.

"Oh I hope they do," I said. Then I spied the desserts. "Look at all the desserts, Louis" I exclaimed. I could feel my mouth watering from looking at the lush dark chocolate éclairs full of cream.

"Before you eat an éclair, come look at all the pears. We have four hundred different varieties of pears in all shapes and colors from coral to green to yellow. We make fruit sorbets from them and keep the sorbet downstairs in the cold underground rooms of the palace. If this thought makes you feel cold, here is coffee from Venice, tea from Holland and hot chocolate from Spain. If we were older we could drink champagne. France has the best champagne." Louis was proud to say.

"Mommy and Daddy drink champagne, Louis, but I would prefer some hot chocolate. It's my favourite drink. Maybe it would make me dance better, I thought.

Louis nodded his head and said, "Most French people drink hot chocolate at night before they go to sleep."

"Well then I had better wait," I said. I did not want to be sleepy when I danced.

"Who is that man by the buffet table, Louis? He looks so serious. He is not talking to anyone else. What is he doing?"

"Oh, Tomasina, he is not a guest. He is the official taster and must taste everything before I do to make sure no one will try to poison me. He has a very

important job. He cannot join into the festivities.
I have some enemics, who might not want me to
be king. A prince or a king must always be very
careful not to be poisoned."

"I am glad no one wants to poison me," I said,
aware that a prince's or king's life was not as easy
as it seemed.

We walked past the buffet. I saw the guests holding
their own spoons and knifes, standing in a line.

"Where are their forks?,"I said. "How can your guests
eat without forks?"

"Oh," said Louis, "forks are very new and not many
people have them yet. However, I do", and Louis
brought a silver fork wrapped in a crisp white linen
napkin out of his pocket.

I looked over at the stage and saw all the men in the
orchestra bowing at their waists towards Louis.

He understood my puzzled gaze and said,"They are
bowing to me because the guests want to begin the
minuet after they finish eating. First they bow to me,
and then they bow to each other and begin
the dance."

I looked all around the Hall of Mirrors and saw the

magnificent costumes, which the gentlemen and ladies were wearing. I was surprised at all the bright colors on everyone, even the men.

Then I noticed that many people had masks covering their eyes. The masks were decorated with sequins and glitter, which made them sparkle under the chandeliers.

"Why are your guests wearing masks, Louis?" I asked.

"The only time commoners are allowed to go to balls at Versailles is if they are masked", he replied." Everyone wants to come here to enjoy all the elegance so they can come if they are masked for a masked ball, like tonight."

"Oh, they must be so excited to be here, Louis. But what is a commoner?" I had never heard this word before.

"A commoner is a person who does not have a title," he replied.

"Then I am a commoner, "I was puzzled and was worried because I did not have on a mask. Then I looked into my hand, and saw a butterfly mask. The fairy had put it there when I was not looking. I put it over my eyes quickly. Now I felt better.

"You are not a commoner tonight, Tomasina. You are a Princess."

I was enjoying looking at all the ladies. They were wearing long embroidered dresses with ruffles, tassels and lace. The men had velvet capes tossed over their shoulders. Some capes were trimmed with white fur. Maybe it was called ermine? I had marabou on my princess costume but Grandie had told me it looked like ermine.

Some men wore jeweled chains around their necks. I had never seen jewelry on men before.

Grandie had told me sapphires were blue, emeralds were green and rubies were red. I saw all these colored stones on the ladies and gentlemen, plus white ones too. I knew the white ones were diamonds. "I love the jewels, Louis. I guess the ladies are given them by their royal families but where do all the beautiful fabrics for their clothes come from?" I asked.

"Please don't tell anyone this secret, Tomasina, but I own all the fabric mills in France. The fabrics are all made in my factories. I need to make lots of money to run the country and pay for all the expenses of Versailles. My companies must be very successful. So I insist that all people come to Court in elegant clothing, which means they must buy my fabrics to have their clothes made and pay me for them.

Also, I like people to be elegantly dressed when they are in grand surroundings. It is pleasing to the eye and makes me happy. I like people to be clever and amusing too."

"I love pretty clothes. I understand, Louis. I wish people still dressed up today," I replied. "The ladies all look so pretty and smart."

"To dress elegantly today, it would be too expensive today," said Louis."As for looking well, the ladies have been working on how they look for hours. Their maids put beauty spots near their eyes to make their eyes seem larger. The maids apply lots of rouge on their mistresses' cheeks, and put pomade on their lips. The hairdressers even stand on ladders to arrange their wigs because the wigs are so tall."

"Is pomade like lipstick," I asked.

"Yes, Louis replied." See, over there is a duchess named Louise de la Valliere. I made her Duchess de la Valliere. If you are a duchess, you can have your coach lined in crimson. The fabric must hang from the walls and not be attached. Only princes and princesses can have their lining attached. Also, she was then allowed to sit on a stool in court instead of standing for a long time."

There is the beautiful Madame de Montespan. I made her a Marquise. She wore a dress to a ball once embroidered with gold. People said fairies must have made it because no human could have done such delicate embroidery."

I looked up at my fairy doll perched on a high windowsill. She had heard what Louis had said. I winked.

"Over there is Madame de Matignon. She will be my second wife. She is flirting with her fan."

"What does 'flirt' mean?" I asked.

"It means to hold your fan under your eyes and move your eyelashes up and down."

"Louis, could I try to flirt with my fan?"

The fairy had put a fan in my hand and I held it up under my eyes. I tried opening and closing my eyes. I could bat my eyelashes going up and down. It was fun. Then Louis turned to me."Tomasina, are you ready to perform? I shall announce you." Louis held up his hand and said,"Ladies and gentlemen, we have a surprise tonight for you before we start the minuet. We have a special ballet dancer named Tomasina and she is going to dance for you."

The people all looked at me. They turned and whispered to each other then turned back and looked at me again. I could feel my cheeks turning pink. What was I going to do? Would I be able to dance well enough? I felt my legs begin to shake. The orchestra began to play. I could hear the violins and a piano playing. I started to walk into the middle of the room.

The fairy fluttered close to me and whispered into my ear,"Pretend your ballet slippers are magic ones. They will make you dance like a real ballerina."

I hoped she was right. I stood on my toes and began to spin slowly around, looking at the fairy on each turn so I would not get dizzy. Around and around I went.

Somehow, the slippers were magical because I began

spinning around, faster and faster, faster than
I had ever done before. I felt like a ballerina from the
Nutcracker Ballet. I was better than I had ever been
in ballet class. Round and round I twirled.

The ladies and gentlemen began
to clap and Louis shouted,"
Bravo, Tomasina."

I looked up at the murals on
the ceiling. I thanked heaven
and the fairy. I could not
believe it but I was a
success. I walked back
to Louis's side like a
princess, smiling, and
slowly bowed gracefully
from my waist.

"You are a star tonight
and a princess too,
Tomasina. He tipped
his head down
towards me.

Chapter 6

We were alone in the Hall of Mirrors. I was back in my nightgown on the throne.

I looked at him. "Louis, you have made my dream come true. You have taught me to be a princess and taken me to a real ball. When I tell my friends about tonight, they will never believe me so I will keep tonight our secret, but it is getting late and I am very tired. I just wanted to go home. I hope you understand." Louis put his hand on my shoulder and smiled, "Of course I understand. I will return. I know where to come to find you now in your little Hall of Mirrors."

"Is that a promise?" I asked.

"Oh, but of course and I always tell the truth."

Bibliography

I.   **Louis XIV and his Court**
by Tom Tierne

II.   **Love and Louis XIV**
by Antonia Fraser

III.   **Madame de Matignon**
byVeronica Buckley

IV.   **Palaces of the Sun King**
by Andrew Zega and Bernd H.Dams

V.   **The Essence of Style**
by Joan de Jean

VI.   **Versailles**
by Tony Spawforth

VII.   **Versailles and the Trianons**
by G.Van Der Kemp and .J.Levron

VIII.   **The Sun King and His Loves**
by Lucy Norton

Robert Dawson and How the Hall of Mirros was Made

A long time ago I was fortunate enough to have a father who enjoyed sticking model kits of boats and planes together for his son, along with a garage and a dolls house from Hobbies Magazine for my sister. I remember watching him stick brick paper to the exterior and painting the windows with enamel paint!

When not keeping his children entertained, he worked in television and would often take me in to the studios to wander around the magical scenery. Of course I ended up working in the theatre and trained as a set designer, while trying to justify my delight in model making with the realities of real life.

In 1988 I formed The Model room, making miniatures for both the theatre and for architects. A chance visit to the Covent Garden Dolls House Shop in London, followed by a visit to Caroline Hamilton who was then running the London Dollhouse Festival resulted in our first commissions for the miniatures market. Nina Eklund, my wife, offered her abilities as a great painter, particularly of faux marble, and we have over the years been incredibly lucky to have the opportunity of making some of the greatest buildings and palaces of the world, including the Vatican, the Doges Palace, the Catherine Palace and Versailles.

The most famous room in Versailles, the Hall of Mirrors, is a particular challenge but always a delightful and fascinating one for us. We have now built three versions of this room, all very different and showing the Hall from a different perspective, both visually and in context. Of course the first challenge is how to achieve any sense of the grandeur of this vast Hall, given that, if modeled in its' entirety, it would measure over 19 feet in length! Luckily for us, it seems to me that the greatness of the Hall is partly due to the rivalry between its' two creators, Marisart the architect and Le Brun the painter, and the result was that every detail of the hall is thought through and a delight in itself, simply magnified by multiplication down the length of the hall, and therefore by showing any one section of the Hall, we are showing the whole in microcosm.

For us, the first stage of any project is to gather all the pictorial reference we can lay our hands on, along with, ideally a visit to get a sense of the particular atmosphere of a space. And Versailles, and the Hall of Mirrors in particular, is full of atmosphere and history, which can be sensed even among the thousands of tourists who daily tread through it.

With the reference around us, working drawings are prepared, both of the overall scheme and of the many of the individual components. It seems to me that the real trick of the miniaturist, if there is one, is to be able to break down any space or object into smaller simpler shapes and forms that can be modeled.

Once this is done, master patterns of capitals, cornices, trophies and the countless other details are fashioned, a silicon mould made from these patterns and resin casts taken so as to be able to produce per-fect copies of the details. These are then painted, or gilded with gold leaf. Walls and pilasters are prepared and painted to look like the fa-mous marble and finally all is put together. The mirror on the doors is actually special optically prepared polished aluminum, each pane cut to shape and positioned.

A fascinating challenge was to recreate some of the silver furniture from the scant surviving drawings and engravings. There is a particular thrill in being able to see an item such as the King's Throne come to life and to be able to view the Hall once more in a way unseen for 350 years.

Finally, all is in place, the parquet floor is waxed and the candles of the chandeliers lit. Louis XIV is reported to have said "Versailles, c'est moi" I think most miniaturists feel the same of their work.